Belondweg Blossoming

For Carla, Pam, and Linda —
My Athena, Artemis, and Aphrodite

For my fragmented family –
My broken mirror

And for Scott –
Whom I love best of all

~Amy Unbounded~

Belondweg Blossoming

ಹಿ⳩

Written and illustrated by
Rachel Hartman

Introduction by
Linda Medley

Production assistance by
Lisa Hurley

ಹಿ⳩

ಹಿ *Pug House Press* ⳩

The author would like to thank the Xeric Foundation for their generous support.

Printed and bound in Canada, home of the Sudbury Neutrino Observatory.

Published by Pug House Press, 250 E. Wynnewood Rd. #E-13, Wynnewood, PA 19096. See our website at *www.amyunbounded.com* or e-mail us at *amyunbounded@yahoo.com*

ISBN# 0-9717900-0-0

First Printing: April 2002
     10 9 8 7 6 5 4 3 2 1

This is a work of fiction, and all characters and situations herein are nothing but the product of my little brain. Resemblance to any non-fictional persons, living or dead, is coincidental.

ℰ𝒪 *Foreword* ᑫ𝓇

By Linda Medley

Several years ago, on a trip back to my family home, I was feeling nostalgic and decided to dig out a bunch of my favorite old childhood books. My mom took one from the top of the stack, contemplating the cover long and hard before returning it.

"You know," she said, in a conspiratorial tone of bitter disgust, "Jo *should've* married LAURIE. Not that – that OLD MAN!"

Right on. Louisa May Alcott's *Little Women* has been a classic of American young adult literature since virtually the day it was first published, in 1868 (Note: modern editions usually combine *Little Women* with its first sequel, *Good Wives*). I don't need to explain or summarize the story; we've all read it. It's been required reading for every generation of American girls since the turn of LAST century. But at some point, *Little Women* started letting us girls down.

Don't get me wrong: it's a great book, an enduring story, and the heroines are wonderfully human. Who *didn't* love Jo, or want to *be* Jo? Wild-haired, spirited, strong-minded, independent, yearning to find fame and fortune as a writer; a budding young feminist if there ever was one. Alcott herself was a feminist, back when feminism was being invented. But she was also the product of the Victorian era, a minister's daughter, and an author with a prim Victorian audience to please. What was expected of young women in Alcott's day – a staggering amount of sweetness and piety, for starters – just isn't expected of today's young girls. Or even desirable. Jo struggles to curb her exuberant nature, and eventually "succeeds," winning the love and support of a stodgy old dope who helps her keep in line. Bah! Pardon me while I avert my disappointed eyes. We may not all have wanted Jo to marry Laurie, but we certainly all wanted Jo to be Jo, to be true to herself, to stand up to and win over the world – not knuckle under to it. I wonder … just how much modern feminist literature has sprouted from generations' worth of unconsciously felt, deep-rooted adolescent disappointment in Jo's fate? Ethno-anthro-spamthropologists could have a field day with that one.

Heh.

Which brings me to a certain other wild-haired, spirited, strong-minded, independent young heroine – one, I think, better suited for our post-modern times. Like Jo March, Amy of Eddybrook Lodge is on the verge of growing up, beginning to see her world with different eyes, feel her world with a different heart. Unlike Jo, however, it's hard to imagine Amy's mother Nahulla ever remonstrating her for losing her temper or defying convention. Speaking up and expressing well-founded moral outrage is something we could all do a little more of, and so is facing challenges with humor, invention and quiet courage as Amy's father Bob does.

No surprise, then, that Amy is Unbounded. I looked up "unbounded" in the dictionary for you, and here's what it says: "1. Having no boundaries or limits. 2. Not kept within bounds; uncontrolled; unrestrained." This is a good thing for Amy, as she is beginning to realize life is a complex undertaking – not always easy, not always happy. But Amy lives life with unbounded spirit and enthusiasm that wins over crotchety old widows, reserved businesswomen, and even makes a careless dragon face the consequences of his actions, when nothing else can. (No doubt it would keep stodgy old German professors at bay as well, were one to inexplicably rear its dopey head!) Living life with an unbounded spirit and enthusiasm is something else we could all do a little more of.

Here's to the turn of a new century, to new heroines and new literature classics, and to being unbounded.

Linda Medley,
January 2002

DRAMATIS PERSONAE:

AS ANYONE WHO'S REACHED THE RIPE OLD AGE OF NINE CAN TELL YOU...

YOU DON'T GET THIS FAR IN LIFE

WITHOUT HAVING PLENTY OF ADVENTURES.

THIS IS **AMY** OUR HEROINE.

AMY'S MOTHER —

Nahulla

IS A BARBARIAN OF THE NORTHERN RUPA' TRIBE. DURING THE 14 YEARS SHE'S LIVED IN GOREDD, SHE HAS TAUGHT HERSELF TO READ, TO MAKE CLOCKS, AND TO BLEND IN PERFECTLY. ER... ALMOST.

AMY'S FATHER —

Bob

IS A WEAVER. HE LIVES HAPPILY AT EDDYBROOK FARM WITH HIS WIFE AND DAUGHTER AND FIFTY-THREE LOWLAND BERGNAL SHEEP.

BOB'S UNCLE —

Sir Cuthberte Pettibone

WAS A THRICE-DECORATED KNIGHT OF THE ORDER OF THE RAMPANT RABBIT BEFORE ALL THE GOREDDI KNIGHTS WERE BANISHED. HE NOW LIVES IN A MUDDY CAVE. YOU'RE NOT SUPPOSED TO KNOW THAT.

SIR CUTHBERTE'S SQUIRE —

Maurizio Vizente Yann-Fañch St. Bazille de Foughfaugh

WAS BANISHED ALONG WITH HIS MASTER SOME 20 YEARS AGO. THEY HAVE DINNER AT EDDYBROOK ONCE A WEEK. FOUGHFAUGH IS A GREAT FAVORITE OF AMY'S.

THE FIRST FARM EAST OF EDDYBROOK IS CALLED NEWGROVE. IT IS HOME TO THE DUCANAHAN FAMILY:

CULLEN

IS THE OLDEST OF THE EIGHT DUCANAHAN SIBLINGS. HE HAS BEEN RUNNING THE FARM SINCE THEIR PARENTS DIED, ALMOST 10 YEARS AGO.

NIALL

IS THE SECOND BROTHER. HE WAS GIVEN TO THE CHURCH AS AN OBLATE AT AGE SEVEN. HE IS NOW THE PRIEST AT ST. KATHANDA'S, NEAR NEWGROVE.

NIESTA

IS NIALL'S TWIN. SHE MAKES CHEESE AND HELPS CULLEN RUN THE FARM. SHE UNSELFISHLY SAW TO IT THAT HER YOUNGER SISTERS COULD MARRY, AND AS A RESULT MIGHT NEVER GET MARRIED HERSELF.

TRIGARTH,

CALLED "TRIG," IS BOB'S APPRENTICE AND SHEPHERD. HE IS PICTURED HERE WITH HIS SAMSAMESE COLLIE — TRIMBLE.

AND THEN THERE'S

BRAN,

THE YOUNGEST DUCANAHAN. HE'S THE SAME AGE AS AMY, AND IS QUITE POSSIBLY HER BEST FRIEND. NOT THAT SHE'D EVER ADMIT THAT, OF COURSE.

NOT PICTURED:

3 MARRIED SISTERS: MAUREEN, JANINE, + DINEEN

Other friends:

DAME OKRA CARMINE, THE NINYAN AMBASSADOR, GAVE AMY HER COPY OF "BELONDWEG."

THE DRAGON LALO FIRST MET AMY WHEN HE WAS DOING AN INTERNSHIP AT THE PALACE. HE PROMISED TO VISIT HER, BUT HASN'T YET.

MOLLY BUTCHER AND **SUSA MELONIO** ARE AMY'S TWO BEST GIRLFRIENDS. THEY LIVE IN LAVONDAVILLE. SUSA MET FOUGHFAUGH ONCE AND HAS **SUCH** A CRUSH ON HIM.

LOUCA AND **PHYLLIDA MALOU** ARE TRAVELING MUSICIANS FROM DISTANT PORPHYRY. THEY COME TO GOREDD EVERY SUMMER.

PAU-HENOA, KNOWN ALSO AS "HEN-WEE" AND "THE MAD BUN," IS A MYTHICAL RABBIT TRICKSTER. HE SUPPOSEDLY HELPED BELONDWEG UNITE GOREDD.

BELONDWEG WOULD HAVE LIVED 1000 YEARS BEFORE AMY, BUT IT IS UNCLEAR WHETHER SHE REALLY EXISTED. HER EXPLOITS ARE THE SUBJECT OF "BELONDWEG," THE NATIONAL EPIC OF GOREDD.

Chapter 1

On the Verge of Summer

In which begins a chronicle of Amy's tenth summer, and Bran behaves better than might have been expected.

...[The] curtain moved
And I beheld her there, a slender girl
Perched just upon the brink of womanhood,
Like the sun on the verge of summer –
Not yet come into her power.

Belondweg, book XVII
The Confession of General Orison

I SING, ye Gods, of **BELONDWEG**
our sure, our strong, our saucy queen,
who fought the haughty Mordondey!
Beside her fought Pau-Henoa.

He glimpsed her first across the plain—
A girl, a wisp, our not-yet queen—
Pentrach's Dun, her father's golden city,
Flamed on the hilltop, Pentrach's Pyre,
her people scattered, captured, dead.
She wept and vowed she would begin again.

So, wait—
AM I SOME
KIND OF **BUNNY**
RABBIT?

PAU-HENOA WAS A RABBIT, YES.

AND HE'S ONE OF THE CLEVEREST HEROES OF...

A RABBIT? IN A **DRESS**?!?

WE WERE IN THE MIDDLE OF A READING LESSON WHEN FATHER NIALL WAS CALLED TO THE BEDSIDE OF EUGENIA LIMEWATER. SHE'S HAD THE FEVER— IT WASN'T UNEXPECTED. "SIT TIGHT," HE SAID, GATHERING HIS HOLY WATER AND A SPRIG OF LAVENDER. "STUDY. I WON'T BE LONG."

BUT MAKING BRAN SIT STILL IS LIKE TRYING TO PUT THE LID BACK ON A BUCKET OF BEES.

YOU'VE OBVIOUSLY MISTAKEN ME FOR SOME SISSYBOY.

AW C'MON! YOU'VE GOTTA ADMIT THIS IS BETTER THAN READING MISTRESS EDWINA'S MANNER BOOKS!

On The Verge of Summer

NIALL'S CHURCH IS ALSO THE SHRINE OF ST. KATHANDA. IT SITS WITHIN A CIRCLE OF STONES CALLED (RESPECTFULLY) "ST. KATY'S TEETH."

THIS WAS A MAJOR PILGRIMAGE SITE ONCE — NOW IT'S JUST A SLEEPY COUNTRY CHURCH. PILGRIMS ARE FICKLE, I GUESS.

THEY SAY ST. KATY USED TO MAKE FLOCKS OF DUCKS DESCEND UPON EVIL DOERS AND QUACK THEM INTO REPENTANCE. HENCE THE OLD SAYING "HE'S DUE FOR DUCKS." NOBODY BUT UNCLE CUTHBERTE ACTUALLY SAYS THAT ANYMORE.

COMPARED TO UNCLE CUTHBERTE, TEN IS NOTHING LIKE OLD.

FIND ANY?

NOPE.

I DON'T GET IT — THERE'S ALWAYS TOADS BETWEEN ST. KATY'S TEETH.

SHE MUST'VE STARTED FLOSSING.

HA-HA— HEY!

HEY WHAT?

THERE'S SOMETHING EVEN BETTER THAN TOADS IN THE CHURCH!

I KNOW WHERE NIALL HIDES THE KEY!

WHAT IS IT?

YOU'LL SEE.

NIALL'S CHURCH IS AS ORDERLY AS HIS HERB GARDEN. HE PERFORMS SERVICES ON MAJOR FEAST DAYS AND ON THE LONG HIGH HOLIDAYS — NOT EVERY DAY LIKE AT ST. GOBNAIT'S IN LAVONDAVILLE. WHICH IS JUST AS WELL, SINCE HIS PARISH IS MADE UP MOSTLY OF SCATTERED FARM FAMILIES, SOME OF WHOM (MY DA) CAN HARDLY REMEMBER WHEN THE LONG HIGH HOLIDAYS **ARE.**

20

21

22

HEY LOOK! YOU CAN SEE HIM THROUGH HERE.

GAH! NIALL'S GONNA KILL ME! PEOPLE ARE ALWAYS SWIPING THE DUCKS FROM THE ALTAR!

HEH.

HEH-HEH!

HM. PAINTED TRYPTICH. VERY LITTLE ORNAMENT. CANDLES.

. . . .

LOTS OF CANDLES.

APPLEWOOD BRANCH. A VESTIGE OF SOME ANCIENT FERTILITY RITE, NO DOUBT.

. . . .

LITTLE STONE DUCKS...

26

29

31

32

KRA-A-TOOM!

SHE'S GONNA GET SOAKED.

THE STORM HAD COME FROM NOWHERE. I COULDN'T EVEN REMEMBER SEEING CLOUDS EARLIER.

BRAN WAS SWALLOWED RIGHT UP BY THE RAIN, DISSOLVED, GONE...

MY BOOK!

I BELIEVE THIS IS YOURS.

OH THANK ALLSAINTS.

BE MORE CAREFUL, EH?

THANKS. I... THANKS.

BELONOWEG

EXCELLENT SCHOLARLY EDITION, THAT. TOP-NOTCH COMMENTARY.

OK! OK!

BELONOWEG

SCHOLARLY BITS BY THE DRAGON LALO

YOU DON'T RECOGNIZE ME, DO YOU.

NO...

I NEVER MET ANY MR. OLLPHEIST BEFORE.

YOU STILL HAVEN'T.

HUH?

AH, DON'T FRET, YOUNG ONE. YOU'LL HAVE ME FIGURED OUT BEFORE THE DAY IS UP, I'M SURE.

BRAN SAID YOU WERE A SCHOLAR.

BRAN WAS RIGHT.

OF ETHNO... UH... ANTHRO...

ETHNOLOGY WAS MY UNDERGRADUATE FIELD. I STUDY HISTORY NOW. THAT'S WHAT BRINGS ME TO YOUR CORNER OF GOREDD.

I WISH TO CONDUCT SOME FIELD RESEARCH.

I HOPED YOUR "FATHER NIALL" WOULD BE ABLE TO RECOMMEND ME A PLACE TO STAY — PARISH PRIESTS OFTEN KNOW THESE THINGS.

35

I WISH I COULD TELL YOU THAT I HAD A SENSE OF FOREBODING THEN, THAT I SAW THE CHANCE MEETING OF LALO AND NIESTA AS A PRELUDE TO THE WHOLE SUMMER, THAT I FOUND THE STORM A BETTER INDICATOR OF THINGS TO COME THAN BRAN'S AIRY PREDICTIONS.

BUT I'M NOT A PARTICULARLY GOOD GUESSER.

I WAS JUST GRATEFUL MY BOOK HAD BEEN SAVED FROM THE RAIN, AND THAT I HAD A LITTLE TIME TO SEE HOW BELONDWEG WAS DOING, WHOSE PROBLEMS SEEMED SO MUCH MORE PRESSING THAN MY OWN...

She made her way to Gealta Glen, the designated rendezvous, To see which of her generals lived and which had fallen through...

Chapter 2

Among Women

Wherein Amy and Mr. Ollpheist
spend a good deal of time with...
oh, take a wild flying guess, why don't you.

Go thy way like Belondweg –
Among women and men.

Folk saying

IT WAS MA WHO THOUGHT OF THE WIDOW SAMPANDER'S. LALO WAS OVERJOYED— IT WAS THE PERFECT HEADQUARTERS FOR A PERIPATETIC RESEARCHER LIKE HIMSELF. DA SAID "PERIPATETIC" MEANS "PICKING PERIWINKLES ON PATIOS," WHICH I TOOK TO MEAN THAT DA DOESN'T KNOW THAT WORD EITHER. PERIWINKLES. **RIGHT.**
I WAS RECRUITED TO HELP "MR. OLLPHEIST" MOVE IN.

AN WHEN THE CHICKENS BECOME TOO NUMBERSOME, YOU JUST SHOO 'EM ON OUT, MR. OLLPHEIST.

YOU ARE ALL GOOD-HEARTED CONSIDERATION, LOBELIA.

BAWK!

YOU'VE EARNED A SCHOLAR'S GRATITUDE.

HEE!

YOU FANCY-FLIRTIN' FURRINER! BE GLAD I'M TOO OLD TO TAKE YOU SERIOUS!

39

Among Women

ON THURSDAY WE WERE AT NEWGROVE HELPING NIESTA PICKLE VEGETABLES.

...SO TOMORROW I TAKE HIM TO MEET PEARL-AGNES.

SORRY? WHO?

NOT THERE, HANH?

SORRY. I'M A BIT... DISTRACTED. MY SISTERS ARE COMING HOME FOR HOLY-MOW...

ALL THREE?

AND THEIR HUSBANDS, **AND** THEIR CHILDREN. I AM **NOT** LOOKING FOR WARD TO THIS.

=SNORT=

YOU HAVE A MONTH!

I HAVE THREE WEEKS.

WELL, ALWAYS YOU CAN BORROW MY AMY.

ISN'T THAT YOUR BIRTHDAY? HOLY-MOW?

YUP. 'CAUSE I'M SO SAINTLY.

STOP, BRAN, OR YOU'RE GONNA CHOP ONIONS.

45

46

TRIG'S SEVENTEEN, BUT YOU WOULDN'T GUESS IT — HE'S SUCH A GOOFUS.

PUT ME DOWN, YOU BIG CLOD!

CLOD, AM I? WHELL.... LOOKY!

I JUST TURNED THE WHOLE WORLD UPSIDE-DOWN!

HA-HA!

SO YOU'D BETTER BE NICE TO ME, OR I MAY JUST LIKE TO LEAVE IT THAT WAY.

HA HA HA! OKAY, OKAY!

SOON WE FORGOT ALL ABOUT THE DRAMA IN THE KITCHEN. TRIG HAD INDEED LANDED US SAFELY BACK ON OUR FEET.

ME NEXT!

HA HA!

HE ALSO APPARENTLY FORGOT THE BIG PILE OF WOOL HE SHOULD HAVE BEEN CARDING. DA MADE **ME** DO IT WHEN I GOT HOME. REMIND ME NOT TO DISTRACT TRIG EVER AGAIN.

WHO NEEDS AN APPRENTICE WHEN YOU'VE GOT A DAUGHTER!

PEARL-AGNES FORTELLGA IS POSSIBLY THE WEALTHIEST TEXTILE MERCHANT IN LAVONDAVILLE. AFTER THE QUEEN, SHE IS PROBABLY THE MOST POWERFUL WOMAN IN GOREDD. I WISH THAT WERE SAYING MUCH...

49

I WILL ALWAYS REMEMBER HIS FACE AT THAT MOMENT, TRANSFIXED, FULL OF CERTAINTY THAT THERE WAS NO PLACE ON EARTH HE'D RATHER BE THAN RIGHT HERE.

HIS REPLY COULDN'T HAVE BEEN MORE PERFECT IF HE'D HAD A HUNDRED YEARS TO THINK ABOUT IT.

"WHERE WOMEN ARE THERE SHALL YOU FIND HEN-WEE; THE WISE CHILD WOULD SIT AT THEIR FEET AND LEARN, THE FOOLISH SEEK TO FLEE."

THAT'S FROM PAU-HENOA'S RETORT TO KING DORDVEIL IN BOOK 6.

AMY'S GOT HER COPY. LET US SEE IT A MINUTE, SWEETIE.

HA! HA! HE'S GOOD.

I TRIED TO TELL YOU. I WOULD HAVE VOUCHED FOR HIM ALL BY MYSELF.

OH RIGHT—BECAUSE HE'S BEEN AT COURT. WELL OL' FARTOLO'S BEEN THERE TOO AND IT DIDN'T DO HIM A LICK OF GOOD!

BARTOLO. DON'T BE CRUDE IN FRONT OF THE CHILD.

53

AT LAST! I FEARED YOU WERE SOME TROUBLE, PERHAPS.

YOU ARE WELCOME, SCHOLAR. MY KITCHEN LEGION DIDN'T GIVE YOU TOO MUCH GRIEF, I HOPE.

PEARLNA, I PRESENT TO YOU MR. OLLPHEIST, THE SCHOLAR.

PEARL-AGNES ALWAYS LOOKS AT YOUR CLOTHES FIRST.

WHICH SCHOLARLY DICTATE SAYS YOU MUST ALL DRESS LIKE GRANDPAS?

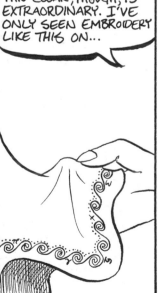

MA SAYS SHE'S SILLY, THAT A GOAT CAN WEAR A BARONET'S HOUPPELAND.

THIS CLOAK, THOUGH, IS EXTRAORDINARY. I'VE ONLY SEEN EMBROIDERY LIKE THIS ON...

BUT THIS TIME IT SERVED HER WELL, AND SHE CAME AWAY KNOWING WHAT MA HADN'T EVEN GUESSED.

OH. OF COURSE! EXCUSE ME!

LALO TOLD PEARL-AGNES ABOUT HIS RESEARCH. MOIRA BROUGHT US TEA. I WAS GRATEFUL.

THAT SOUNDS FASCINATING!

BLAH BLAH BLAH.

I THINK YOU'LL FIND THAT EVEN ILLITERATE GOREDDI WOMEN CAN RECITE CERTAIN PASSAGES FROM BELONDWEG BY HEART.

I WOULD VERY MUCH LIKE...

TO INTERVIEW SOME OF THE WOMEN WHO GATHER IN YOUR KITCHEN.

YOU ARE WELCOME TO DO SO, OF COURSE.

AND TO INTERVIEW YOU, IF I MAY.

OH POOH! I WOULD BE USELESS IN AN INTERVIEW.

I'D LOVE TO HEAR ABOUT YOUR TEXTILE BUSINESS.

MORE THAN YOU MIGHT SUPPOSE.

AND WHAT HAS THAT TO DO WITH BELONDWEG?

THERE'S NOT MUCH TO SAY. IT IS A GOOD BUSINESS— I HAVE PROSPERED BY IT.

IT HARDLY SEEMED FAIR TO GIVE ALL MY HARD WORK OVER TO A HUSBAND, BUT NOW IT SEEMS I SHALL BE GIVING IT OVER TO THE CITY MAGISTRATES INSTEAD.

UNLESS I CAN GET SPECIAL DISPENSATION FROM THE QUEEN, THE BUSINESS BELONGS TO THE CITY AT THE END OF THIS SUMMER TO DISPOSE OF AS THEY SEE FIT.

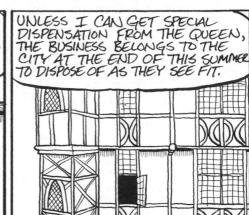

MY MIND HAD BEEN RACING EVER SINCE MA SAID "YOU ARE DRIVEN LIKE SHEEP."

WHO WERE? WOMEN? ALL WOMEN OR JUST SOME OF THEM?

I COULD SEE HOW NIESTA, FOR EXAMPLE, WAS DRIVEN. SHE NEVER GOT TO DO WHAT SHE WANTED.

BUT YOU'D THINK SOMEONE RICH AND INFLUENTIAL WOULD BE FREE TO DRIVE HER OWN FATE.

AND WHAT ABOUT MA? SHE WASN'T A SHEEP. WAS THAT A FLUKE? WAS IT BECAUSE SHE WAS FROM FAR AWAY?

COULD I GROW UP TO BE A FLUKE TOO BECAUSE SHE WAS MY MOTHER?

I WAS VERY SCARED THAT I COULDN'T.

OH, I'VE HAD OFFERS, BUT I CAN'T BRING MYSELF TO SELL JUST YET.

HOW ABOUT OFFERS OF MARRIAGE?

HA! JUST ONE. AN OLD BAT LIKE ME SHOULD BE GRATEFUL, I SUPPOSE. BUT WHERE ARE THE RAPACIOUS FORTUNE-HUNTERS OF YORE?

HMPH!

YAY!

ST. DAAN...

NONA, INFORM YOUR SEAMSTRESSES THAT MEN'S HEMLINES ARE TO GO **DOWN** FOR FALL.

YES MA'AM!

UGH...! **WAY** DOWN.

I AM IN YOUR DEBT. YOU MAY INTERVIEW ME AS OFTEN AS YOU WISH.

UM, YES. UM... NOW YOU KNOW I'M NOT...UM... IN A POSITION TO BE A...

HA-HA! OF COURSE NOT. BUT BARTOLO WON'T KNOW THAT.

YOU WILL FIND THAT GOREDDI WOMEN ARE MANY THINGS...

...BUT WE DON'T TAKE SUIT FROM DRAGONS.

61

MA ASKED HIM TO DINNER THE NEXT DAY AND I WAS SENT TO FETCH HIM. LIKE HE DIDN'T KNOW THE WAY, YOU'RE THINKING. YAH, OKAY, I VOLUNTEERED.

...AND IT'S STILL BOTHERING ME.

HM. MY INTERPRETATION OF THAT PARTICULAR LINE WAS THAT YOUR MA'S HOMESICK.

HOME-SICK?

WELL, THINK ABOUT IT. AMONG HER PEOPLE, WOMEN AREN'T JUST FREE, THEY'RE IN CHARGE. EVEN LIVING IN A HOUSE MUST SEEM CONFINING TO HER NOMAD'S HEART. NO WONDER SHE FEELS LIKE A HERDED SHEEP.

WHICH IS NOT TO SAY, UNFORTUNATELY, THAT SHE WAS ENTIRELY WRONG. BUT COMPARED TO NINY'S AND SAMSAM, GOREDDI WOMEN DO PRETTY WELL.

WHY, WE RAN ACROSS A WHOLE KITCHEN FULL OF NOT-SO-SHEEPISH WOMEN— NOT ALL GOREDDI, I ADMIT, BUT ALL CONTRIBUTING TO GOREDD.

YOU WON'T FIND THE LIKES OF NONA IN SAMSAM. AND THAT DOSEY! WE HAVE **GOT** TO GET HER PACKED OFF TO UNIVERSITY.

WE?

I MEAN... AW, CACK!

HE MEANS LARRY! LARRY OLLPHEIST!

YOU'RE NOT HELPING, AMY.

LALO'S NICER. LIKE THE SOUND OF WATER. KEEP THAT ONE.

WHAT'S ALL THE GRAPE-VINE FOR?

HOLY-MOW WREATHS. ASK YOUR MA IF YOU CAN HELP ME A COUPLE AFTERNOONS NEXT WEEK.

I COULD COME HELP TOO, THEN IT'D ONLY TAKE ONE AFTERNOON.

DON'T YOU HAVE WORK OF YOUR OWN TO DO?

AH, BUT I COULD DO MY WORK AT THE SAME TIME...

I ROLLED MY EYES. HE OBVIOUSLY DIDN'T KNOW THAT YOU CAN'T MAKE SOMEONE LIKE YOU BY SHOWING HER YOUR BORING SIDE FIRST.

TELL ME SOMETHING, NIESTA. DID YOUR MOTHER TELL YOU STORIES...

THEN AGAIN, IF BORING'S ALL YOU'VE GOT...

I WAS SURE HE'D LOST HER. NIESTA GETS SKEPTICAL IF YOU TALK TO HER TOO MUCH.

IT MUST MEAN YOU WANT SOMETHING. SEE THOSE HARD SHOULDERS? SKEPTICAL.

THEN I SAW HER FACE.

I NEVER KNEW THAT EXPRESSION WAS IN HER VOCABULARY.

ALMOST IMPERCEPTIBLY THOUGH, SOMETHING BEGAN TO CHANGE.

SHE WAS... INTERESTED.

66

67

I COULD HARDLY CONTAIN MYSELF THE REST OF THE WAY HOME. LOOK FOR DOORS, HE'D SAID. WELL HE **WAS** THE DOOR, FOR NIESTA ANYWAY. HE WOULD BE HER PAU-HENOA.

SHE DIDN'T NEED TO KNOW HE WAS A DRAGON, I DECIDED. IT WOULD JUST FREAK HER OUT. THE REAL PAU-HENOA HADN'T BEEN HUMAN EITHER. SO THERE.

LALO SEEMED ABLE TO PULL ANY OF US BACK FROM THE BRINK OF CHAOS, TO SOOTHE THE SAVAGE SAMPANDER AND BOLSTER THE FLAGGING FORTELLGA, TO UNDERSTAND MA AND SEND DOSEY TO UNIVERSITY. I WANTED TO BE JUST LIKE HIM.

IT WASN'T A BAD THING TO BE A GIRL. LALO BELIEVED IN US.

AND SUDDENLY THE WORLD SEEMED POSSIBLE AGAIN. I COULD BARELY CONTAIN MYSELF. I WAS FULL OF ZAZMINI, AS MA WOULD SAY. FULL OF GRASSHOPPERS.

Chapter 3

And Men

Which is chock-full of hay mowing,
leek harvesting, bulging biceps and bad news.

They gazed upon me one last time, those eyes...
Now rimmed in red. "O Belondweg," he said,
"Forget not that your father loved you."
Then fled his spirit, eager for the stars.

Belondweg, book IV
The Sorrows

And Men

DA HAD BEEN KIND OF PREOCCUPIED SINCE SPRING.

UH-HUH. PANTA -- WHAT?

I WASN'T SURE WHY. I DID MY BEST TO MAKE HIM LAUGH, AND HOPED IT HELPED.

JUST WRAP 'EM AROUND...

AND WEAR 'EM TO WAR!

HEH-HEH.

BUT WAR'S TOO MESSY. WASTE OF GOOD WOOL.

I'VE BEEN READING BELONDWEG, AS YOU KNOW. SHE WAS FOND OF HER DA, TOO.

HERE. WHAT IF YOU MADE IT INTO WINGS.

HE DIES BEFORE THE START OF THE BOOK.

CHIRP! CHIRP!

SEE, THAT'S MUCH MORE...

AW, NUTS.

gallop! gallop!

SHE TELLS PAU-HENOA HOW SHE FOUGHT THE MORDONDEY BY HIS SIDE...

WHO IS IT, DA? WHO IS IT?

HOW HIS RETAINERS HAD TO DRAG HER AWAY AFTER HE HAD FALLEN...

ROBERDT ARDHOUSE?

FRIENDS CALL ME BOB.

73

74

MMN?

IT'S STILL YOUR TURN, SQUIRREL-BAIT.

ER... I JUST FLANKED YOUR BROOD WITH MY LESSER CRUB, IF THAT HELPS.

UHM, O-KAY. TWO SMALL DETAILS — 1) THAT'S NOT A MOVE (AT LEAST, NOT A MOVE YOU KNOW YET), SO LET'S PUT IT BACK.

AND 2) WHAT'S HAPPENING OVER THERE ISN'T YOUR PROBLEM, ALL RIGHT? THE BIG KIDS'LL WORK IT OUT.

SORRY. SORRY. I'M JUST...

A LITTLE WORRY-WART?

OR SOMETHING. WHY CAN'T DA TAKE HIS WORK TO SHOPS IN TOWN?

HE'S NOT IN THE GUILD.

NOW THE SHOPKEEPERS COULD SEND SOMEONE OUT TO **HIM**, BUT THEY WON'T. TOO MUCH EFFORT FOR TOO LITTLE RETURN.

The rent is paid in blankets...

The clocks bring in something...

a daughter, for ke! She'll be a dowry one days!

79

WHO TOLD YOU THAT?

MY FRIEND SUSA.

THE MELLONIO GIRL? HEH-HEH.

WHAT?

SHE WROTE ME A RATHER... MUSHY POEM.

SHE LIKES YOU.

I GATHERED THAT. HOW'D THAT ONE VERSE GO..? "I'LL COMPARE THEE TO A SUMMER'S DAY, THY SMILE LIKE SUNSHINE AND THY HAIR LIKE HAY..."

IT'S ACCURATE AND IT RHYMES.

NOT LIKE I'VE NEVER MADE A FOOL OF MYSELF IN PURSUIT OF A LOST CAUSE. WHEN I WAS SEVEN AND PEARL-AGNES WAS FIFTEEN, I HAD SUCH A CRUSH ON HER, AND I...

OH!

THAT'S IT! THAT'S IT! AMY, YOU MAD GENIUS, YOU!

WHAT? WHAT?

THERE WAS MUCH SLAPPING OF FOREHEADS WHEN FOUGHFAUGH MENTIONED PEARL-AGNES. IT WAS AGREED THAT HE AND MA WOULD GO TO TOWN THE NEXT DAY TO SEEK HER ADVICE.

SHE HASN'T GOT THE CLOUT TO GET YOU REINSTATED.

I WON'T NEED TO BE REINSTATED IF SHE'LL CARRY MY WORK.

81

DA'S NOT ONE TO SIT IDLE WHEN HE'S WORRIED. HARD WORK, HE SAYS, IS GOOD FOR WHATEVER AILS YOU.

HE MUST'VE BEEN PRETTY ANXIOUS ABOUT PEARL-AGNES'S MEETING— WE SPENT THE NEXT THREE AFTERNOONS AT NEWGROVE, HELPING THE DUCANAHANS MOW.

I am a plowboy, the field for to sow, an' that is well-known to my neighbor— 'Tis many a field that I have plowed, an' that without much labor...

THANKS FOR LENDING A HAND.

DON'T MENTION IT, CULLEN. THE SOONER YOUR MEADOW'S MOWN, THE SOONER I GET MY APPRENTICE BACK.

UM...YES. ABOUT THAT... WHAT'S THIS I HEAR ABOUT YOU IN SOME KIND OF TROUBLE WITH THE GUILD?

IT'S AGAINST MY DA'S NATURE TO LIE. I COULD SEE HIS JAW WORKING, AS THOUGH HE COULD SOFTEN THE TRUTH BY CHEWING IT. TRIG NOTICED TOO.

AW, CULLEN...

GAH!

IT'S NOTHING, JEALOUSY. IT'LL BLOW OVER IN A FORTNIGHT.

IT BETTER.

I'M GONNA **KILL** THAT CHICKEN-NECKED PRIEST!

NEXT THING I KNEW, EVERYBODY WAS RUNNING. CULLEN TOOK OFF FOR ST. KATHANDA'S WITH DA RIGHT ON HIS HEELS — BRAN RAN THE OTHER WAY SCREAMING FOR TRIG — I JUST FOLLOWED MY FEET, WHICH KNEW WHERE THEY WANTED TO GO BETTER THAN I DID.

VILLAIN!

KNAVE!

CUCKOLD!

NIALL, THIS IS ALL MY FAULT...

NO, NO. I LIED. A LIAR WILL ALWAYS GET WHAT HE DESERVES.

HUFF! PUFF!

DID YOU THINK YOU'D GET AWAY WITH THIS?!?

NOT REALLY. I HOPED I WOULD.

CULLEN! JUST COOL IT, ALL RIGHT?

NIESTA HAS WORKED AS HARD AS YOU. SHE RAISED TRIG AND DINEEN AND BRAN—FROM A BABY!—BUT YOU DON'T EVEN HAVE THE **DECENCY** TO SEE HER SETTLED...

...BEFORE BRINGING IN SOME CALLOW SIXTEEN-YEAR-OLD TO UNDERMINE HER AUTHORITY AND TAKE HER PLACE AT TABLE!

 AWWW...' THE **GOOD** BROTHER HAS SPOKEN.

 THE LOVING BROTHER! THE STELLAR SEMINARY STUDENT WHO COULD HAVE HAD A CATHEDRAL, BUT TOOK A RUN-DOWN COUNTRY CHURCH BECAUSE HE *LOVES* HIS SISTER.'

BECAUSE HE WISHES TO PROTECT HER.

 DO YOU KNOW WHAT HE DID? DO YOU KNOW WHAT THE LITTLE FOOL DID? HE OFFERED TO BUY HER GUARDIANSHIP OFF ME. LIKE I'M DUMB ENOUGH TO PART WITH MY BEST WORKER.

 AND WHAT WOULD HE DO WITH HER? A PRIEST CAN'T KEEP A WOMAN. WOULD HE PUT HER IN A NUNNERY? I CAN'T SEE HER BEING TOO HAPPY THERE. SHE'D MISS HER BOYFRIEND.

 NIESTA HAS A BOYFRIEND?

 NOT THAT **SHE**'D ADMIT TO. BUT I'VE SEEN HOW HE LOOKS AT HER.

HOW DOES HE LOOK AT HER?

88

89

I KNOW NONA OPENS MY MAIL, IF THAT'S THE QUESTION.

PT!

A PERFECT ENDING TO A PERFECT DAY.

HOW WAS THE...

YOU HAVE TO ASK? BAD. VERY VERY BAD.

I DIDN'T REALIZE I WAS SUCH A LAME DUCK. NO ONE WOULD LISTEN — WHY SHOULD THEY IF THEY'RE PLANNING WAYS TO CARVE UP MY PROPERTY? MY WORDS CARRY NO CONSEQUENCE.

NOT EVEN IF I WEAR MY MOST CONSERVATIVE DRESS.

THESE GHASTLY PLEATED CUFFS!

HAZPAH, MY PEARL! WHAT WILL YOU...

AH-AH, NO FRETTING, MY FRIEND. I KEEP MY PROMISES.

I SHALL GET MARRIED.

OH STOP GAPING. I GET TO KEEP THE BUSINESS IF I MARRY, SO I'LL MARRY. WHAT'S HARD ABOUT THIS?

BUT... BUT WHO..?

OH, LET'S SEE. I HAVE TEN MILLION SUITORS, SO I THINK I'LL PICK ...BARTOLO!

SIT DOWN. ALL OF YOU.

YOU CAN'T MARRY BARTOLO!

I CAN AND I WILL.

I'VE THE QUEEN'S CLEAR DISPENSATION IN HAND: HE'S IN NO POSITION TO MAKE DEMANDS. HE SHALL RECEIVE A STIPEND SUFFICIENT TO PAY OFF HIS CREDITORS AND BUY HIMSELF THE OCCASIONAL NEW DOUBLET, AND HE'LL CONSIDER HIMSELF FORTUNATE.

YOU CAN DO THIS WITH SUCH A COLD EYE?!'

IT'S BUSINESS, NAHULLA, NOT ROMANCE.

AND I'M NOT QUITE AS DISPASSIONATE IN THIS AS YOU IMAGINE.

I'VE CONTEMPLATED **NOT** KEEPING THIS UP — SELLING MY SHOPS AND WAREHOUSES AND RETIRING TO SOME QUIET CONVENT WITH A NICE GARDEN.

BUT, EARLY ON ANYWAY, THAT PLAN WOULD ALWAYS GET SNAGGED ON THE MEMORY OF MY FATHER.

HE WAS MY COMPANION, MENTOR AND FRIEND. HE TAUGHT ME TO STAND FIRM, TO BE GENEROUS AND BROAD-MINDED AND SELF-RELIANT... I MISS HIM TERRIBLY.

BUT HE WOULDN'T HAVE WANTED ME TO KEEP THIS UP FOR PURE SENTIMENTALITY, AND ULTIMATELY I HAVEN'T.

IN MEMORIAM

MARCANTONIO FORTELLISA

IF I CLING TO HIS BUSINESS NOW, IT'S BECAUSE I LOVE IT. I'M GOOD AT IT.

THIS LAST WEEK HAS EMPHASIZED TO ME THAT, WHATEVER THE STRUGGLE, I NEED TO KEEP THIS BUSINESS GOING, THAT I HAVE A **DUTY** TO DO SO.

WHERE ELSE CAN SOMEONE LIKE YOUR HUSBAND TURN WHEN REJECTED BY THE GUILD? FORTELLGA'S IS BIG ENOUGH TO TAKE RISKS OTHERS CAN'T.

AH, PEARL, THIS IS STILL FOOLISHNESS..

AS LONG AS MY DOORS ARE OPEN, THERE WILL BE A PLACE FOR THE INDEPENDENT CRAFTER PRODUCING WORK OF GOOD QUALITY.

DA FOUND HER DECISION SOBERING.

I HOPE SHE STILL FEELS THAT WAY AFTER LIVING WITH THAT BOOR FOR A MONTH.

WE CANNOT RE-PAY THIS DEBT, MY BOB.

THERE HAS TO BE SOME WAY OUT, NAHULLA. MAYBE WE **CAN** REPAY HER..

BEFORE SHE WALKS OFF THIS CLIFF FOR US. I'LL SPEAK TO MY UNCLE...

ON, MY CHARGER!

TRIG!

oops

LISTEN, TRIG— THERE'S A GOOD CHANCE I'M NOT GOING TO BE REINSTATED IN THE GUILD AFTER ALL. I'D LOVE TO KEEP YOU ON, BUT I DON'T WANT YOU TO FEEL LIKE YOU HAVE TO STAY.

MY SITUATION WON'T HELP YOUR CAREER ANY— WHICH DOESN'T MEAN YOU COULDN'T DO YOUR JOURNEYMANSHP IN SAMSAM OR NINYS...

UM...

IF IT'S ALL THE SAME TO YOU... I'D JUST AS SOON STAY.

YOU'LL BE WANTING AN EXTRA SET OF HANDS MORE THAN EVER, I RECKON, NOW THAT YOU'RE ON YOUR OWN.

DA SEEMED TOUCHED BY HIS LOYALTY.

I'LL HELP TOO, DA.

YOU NEVER HAD A CHOICE!

NOW SOME PEOPLE MIGHT FIND THAT REMARK TOO SNIPPY, BUT NOT ME. IF HE WAS TEASING ME, IT MEANT THE LAST OF HIS WORRIES HAD FINALLY RELEASED ITS GRIP.

DON'T BE SO SURE. I ALMOST WENT TO JOIN THE SAMSAMESE CIRCUS!

BUT YOU STAYED TO HELP ME TURN THE HAY! WHAT A SWEETHEART!

I ONCE ASKED TRIG IF HE REMEMBERED HIS DA. "OH SURE," HE SAID. "HE WAS LIKE WHAT YOU'D GET IF YOU MIXED TOGETHER THE BEST PARTS OF CULLEN AND NIALL." I DID THE ARITHMETIC AND CAME UP WITH A KINDLY OAF—JUST LIKE TRIG.

I'M A LOT LIKE MY DA TOO, EVEN THOUGH I'M A GIRL AND HE'S A MAN. AND YOU KNOW WHAT, THE WOODS DON'T PART TO LET **HIM** PASS, EITHER. HE'S HAD TO WORK HARD TO FORGE HIS OWN PATH. HE'S NEEDED THE HELP OF OTHERS TO CREATE A PLACE FOR HIMSELF.

I WILL GLADLY ACCOMPANY HIM UP THAT PATH, HELPING WHERE I CAN, AND WHEN IT'S TIME FOR ME TO FORGE MY OWN, I'LL ALREADY BE AN OLD HAND AT IT.

SO I'VE BEEN THINKING ABOUT THESE "PANTALOONS" OF YOURS.

NOT THE WAY **YOU** TIED 'EM, SURE. BUT WHAT IF...

OH, DA! THAT WAS JUST SILLINESS! NOBODY'D WEAR SOMETHING LIKE **THAT**!

Chapter 4

The Flash

**In which Holy-Mow is celebrated,
Fustian cakes are consumed in great quantity,
and our Amy gets a crush on**

I spied her in the glen
As she gathered roses in

She were the sweetest maid
Who had ever graced a glade

In a flash I were struck down
By her eye of softest brown

"Girl, my heart is thine to have
An thy heart be thine to give"

But not a word she said
Oh, she looked on me so sad

And I walk the hills alone
Ever after – she is gone

My black-haired mountain girl, ah!
My black-haired mountain girl, tu-ru!
My black-haired mountain girl!

Base lyrics to *My Black-Haired Mountain Girl*,
as sung in Mews province, Goredd

eadlong, desperately, down the hill's cold face
Plunged Belondweg, through bracken & through thorn,
The hideous thund'rous footsteps in her wake
Of hoardes unseen, the gurgle of the beast,
Her heart enraged at having been betrayed...

IF ONLY I'D LISTENED TO PAU-HENOA!

SLAM!

BIG HANDS PLUCKED ME
OUT OF THE MUCK AND SET ME
GENTLY ON THE WALL, AND
THAT'S WHEN IT HAPPENED—

THE MOMENT I'VE COME TO CALL...

The Flash

THE REST OF THAT EVENING IS KIND OF A BLUR. IT WAS DETERMINED THAT I'D BROKEN MY LITTLE TOE.

THIS IS PARTLY MY FAULT...

SHE'LL BE TEN NEXT WEEK, TRIG. SHE'S OLD ENOUGH TO KNOW BETTER.

AAAAAAAAHH

MA SCOLDED ME.

WHAT YOU WERE THINKING, HANH?!?

KEHAMPAH!

HATAPATA!

DA SCOLDED ME.

I'M DISAPPOINTED. WE'RE TRYING TO RAISE A SENSIBLE GIRL, NOT ONE WHO WANTONLY ENDANGERS HER-SELF!

I WAS TUCKED INTO THE BIG BED DOWNSTAIRS AND SCOLDED ONCE MORE FOR GOOD MEASURE. I DON'T KNOW WHERE MA AND DA SLEPT — IT WAS THEIR BED.

WHAT I DO REMEMBER ABSOLUTELY CLEARLY IS THAT I COULDN'T SLEEP, THAT I TOSSED AND TURNED UNTIL THE MOON WAS HIGH IN THE SKY, BUT NOTHING HELPED.

I COULDN'T STOP THINKING ABOUT TRIG.

IT WAS A PREOCCUPATION

TODAY YOU ARE FOR CHORES INDOORS. NO WALKING, ANH? JUST CHURNING OF BUTTER.

OKAY.

WHAT?

WHICH FOLLOWED ME

WHERE I AM PUTTING THESE BUTTER-MOLDS?

OVER HERE, MA. ON THE TRI※...THE TRAY.

ON THE TRAY.

ALL THAT NEXT DAY...

TRIG... TRIG... TRIG...

HEY! THERE'S HEARTS ON ALL THE BUTTER! MAYBE IT'S A SIGN!

I MADE A POINT OF SITTING BY HIM AT SUPPER.

IF YOU SCOOTED OVER ABOUT SIX INCHES, I COULD EAT WITHOUT ELBOWING YOU IN THE HEAD. HOW DOES THAT SOUND?

AND I KEPT LOOKING FOR "SIGNS."

IF HE TAKES A SECOND HELPING OF BEETS, HE LIKES ME. IF HE BURPS WITHOUT SAYING "EXCUSE ME," HE DOESN'T. IF HE REACHES ACROSS ME FOR BREAD, HE'LL GROW UP TO BE A PIRATE.

COOOL!

OBVIOUS. I CAN'T VOUCH FOR LALO, BUT I SUSPECT THE TRUE QUEEN OF OBVIOUS WAS ME.

THE DAYS FLEW BY. THE WEATHER WAS BEAUTIFUL AND I WAS JOLLY... TRIG DIDN'T STAND A CHANCE.

PASS THE BEETS.

OKAY, MUFFIN-HEAD!

GOOBER!

STINK-WHEAT!

AMYPAH!

I ENGAGED HIM IN WITTY REPARTEE.

...INCHME FELL OFF—WHO WAS LEFT?

OKAY!

PINCHME?

I HELPED HIM WITH HIS WORK.

HA!

I TOOK THE HEAT FOR HIM WHEN HE DIDN'T FINISH.

QUIT DISTRACTING HIM!

108

BUT...
    EITHER HE REALLY DIDN'T NOTICE ANY CHANGE IN MY BEHAVIOR, OR HE CHOSE NOT TO LET ON. KNOWING TRIG, BOTH ARE EQUALLY LIKELY.
    I TRIED ONE LAST BARRAGE OF UNSUBTLETY.

TOMORROW'S MY BIRTHDAY!

YUP.

AND IT'S HOLY-MOW! MY MA TAUGHT ME ALL THE SET DANCES. ARE YOU GONNA DANCE?

YUP.

I'M GONNA DANCE ALL NIGHT! IF YOU'RE LUCKY, I MIGHT EVEN DANCE WITH YOU!

YOUR TOE'S WELL ENOUGH FOR ALL THAT?

AND MYSELF. AHOY!

AND HIS DOG.

I DECORATED HIS SHOES.

UH... THANKS.

111

NIESTA'S YOUNGEST SISTER, DINEEN, MARRIED JOHN DE GRUYON. THAT MEANS SHE MERITS A HALF-CURTSY WHEN SHE ENTERS A ROOM, AS WELL AS A 3-NOTE TRUMPET FLAIR (WHEN AVAILABLE). IF YOU FORGET THE CURTSY, SHE GETS CROSS.

GREETINGS, SISTER.

HULLO!

DINEEN IS... WELL... QUITE A CHALLENGE TO GET ALONG WITH.

THEY HAVE NOT YET MADE US A SUITABLE PLACE TO SIT.

I SENT OLLIE OUT TO CHECK ON IT.

WELL, YOU DIDN'T SEND HIM SOON ENOUGH, DID YOU.

SHE'S ALSO YOUNGER THAN TRIG, WHICH GALLS NIESTA TO NO END.

A MOTHER-TO-BE CAN'T **STAND** ALL NIGHT.

SHE CAN BE SUCH A PILL THAT IT'S EASY TO LOSE SIGHT OF JOHN...

DINDY, LOVE, YOU WAIT HERE AND I'LL GO HELP OUT.

WHO IS, STRANGELY, A FINE FELLOW.

I WORE MY GRUBBIES SO I CAN GO WORK WITH YOUR MENFOLK.

IN THE DIRT.

NEVER MIND THAT HIS "GRUBBIES" COST MORE THAN SOME OF THOSE "MENFOLK" SEE IN A YEAR.

OH! AND I BROUGHT YOU A SURPRISE, SISTER!

TELL HER WHAT IT IS, DINDY.

YOU'RE NOT THE BOSS OF ME!

I AM THE BOSS OF EVERYTHING UNDER THIS ROOF!

I HATE YOU!

GOOD! GET OUT!

I'm telling my *snif* HUSBAND.

FOR A FLEETING SECOND I SAW HIS FACE SOFTEN. I THOUGHT HE WOULD SAY SOMETHING TO NIESTA.

MOST EVERYONE'S HERE. GUESS I'LL GET THINGS STARTED.

FUSTIAN CAKES'LL BE DONE SHORTLY.

OK, SOMETHING NICER THAN **THAT**.

ARE YOU STILL HERE, AMY? I'LL FINISH UP. YOU SHOULD BE OUT HAVING FUN WITH THE OTHER KIDS.

I DIDN'T HAVE TO BE TOLD TWICE. MOLLY AND SUSA WERE ALREADY THERE.

THERE SHE IS!

HURRY UP! THE DANCING JUST STARTED!

DANCING IS THE BEST PART OF HOLY-MOW. GOREDDIS LOVE TO DANCE. THE WORLD COULD BE COMING TO AN END, CHUNKS OF FLAMING SKY FALLING ALL AROUND US, AND YOU'D FIND US TRYING TO SQUEEZE IN ONE LAST DOMPE OR PIVO.

THE WORLD JUST MELTS AWAY WHEN YOU'RE DANCING. IT'S LIKE BEING IN LOVE WITH THE WHOLE WORLD AT ONCE, GIDDY, HAPPY, AND READY TO LOOK LIKE AN UTTER FOOL.

I LIKE **WATCHING** PEOPLE DANCE, TOO. AT LEAST, I HOPE I DO.

I EXPLAINED ABOUT MY TOE.

118

FOOD IS ALMOST AS GOOD AS DANCING, ANYHOW. ALMOST.

I DECIDED TO GET IT OVER WITH.

MY FRIEND SUSA WANTS TO KNOW...

NOPE. UH-UNH.

NO?!?

HE WOULD?

NEVER. YOUR UNCLE WOULD KILL ME.

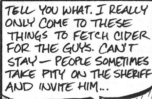

TELL YOU WHAT. I REALLY ONLY COME TO THESE THINGS TO FETCH CIDER FOR THE GUYS. CAN'T STAY — PEOPLE SOMETIMES TAKE PITY ON THE SHERIFF AND INVITE HIM...

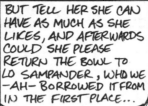

BUT TELL HER SHE CAN HAVE AS MUCH AS SHE LIKES, AND AFTERWARDS COULD SHE PLEASE RETURN THE BOWL TO LO SAMPANDER, WHO WE —AH— BORROWED IT FROM IN THE FIRST PLACE...

WAIT A MINUTE..!

BUT IT WAS TOO LATE.

I WASN'T ASKING ABOUT UNCLE CUTHBERTE'S NASTY ASPIC RECIPE! FOUGHFAUGH! YOU BIG COWARD! COME BACK HERE!

SUSA'S WAITING FOR ME TO BRING HER AN ANSWER!

NOT THAT SUSA WAS PARTICULARLY SUFFERING WHILE SHE WAITED...

≥SIGH≤

FAIR ENOUGH.

YOU SHOULD PICK THE TUNE, AT LEAST.

HOW ABOUT "MY BLACK-HAIRED MOUNTAIN GIRL?"

TWO-FOOT IS WAY TOO STRANGE TO EXPLAIN HERE. IT'S A VERY OLD FORM — NO INSTRUMENTS, JUST TWO GUYS SINGING AND CLAPPING. I THINK ORIGINALLY IT WAS SOME KIND OF CONTEST OF WITS, BUT I DON'T REALLY KNOW. IT'S SOMETHING ELSE YOU CAN ASK LALO IF YOU EVER GET A CHANCE.

SOMEBODY ONCE MARVELLED AT MY MA'S ABILITY TO DANCE A TWO-FOOT. "ARE YOU KIDDING?" ANSWERED DA. "FIRST THING SHE DID WHEN SHE CAME TO GOREDD WAS MAKE ME TEACH HER EVERY DANCE I KNEW."

I spied her in the glen
As she gathered roses in

I spied her in the glen
Glow of summer on her skin

Glow of summer on her skin
Round her neck a daisy chain

As she gathered roses in
Wet with dew or wet with rain

Wet with dew or wet with rain
I will see her there again

I will kiss her on the chin
when I come for her again

NOW WAS MY CHANCE — I'D TALK TO TRIG WHILE HE WASN'T DANCING, AND BE SO FASCINATING THAT HE'D FORGET TO START UP AGAIN.

THERE WAS, OF COURSE, ONE SMALL SNAG IN THE PLAN.

WHERE IN THE WORLD IS HE?

UH...

I HAVE A VAGUE MEMORY OF FLEEING AS FAST AS MY TOE WOULD LET ME...

I can't believe it she came out of OH NO OH NO OH NO *I'm so stupid what was I think* *'s a milkmaid! only ten of course he prefers gi* *way too old for* *is so embarrassing! At least I don't tell ev* *age! I'm such a* *like Susa. Susa! I'm just like Susa! I* nothing bu boys boys boys

AND OF FINDING MYSELF, MYSTERIOUSLY, UNDER NIESTA'S KITCHEN TABLE. I DON'T THINK SHE REALIZED I WAS THERE.

just like her! I'm preoccupi when did this begin? How an I stop? I don't want to him, I want it to be like it was be this was never to me I never boys

HECK, I ONLY REALIZED I WAS THERE WHEN NIALL CAME IN, AFTER WHAT MUST HAVE BEEN QUITE A WHILE.

NIESTA! I'VE COME TO KICK YOU OUT OF THE KITCHEN!

125

WHAT? WHY?

LET'S JUST SAY THAT A CERTAIN GENTLEMAN FRIEND OF YOURS...

WAS ABOUT TO COME IN AND HELP YOU FINISH WHATEVER'S BEEN KEEPING YOU...

WHEN I CLEVERLY PROPOSED THAT **I** SHOULD COME IN, TAKE UP YOUR TASK, AND SEND **YOU** OUT TO **HIM**...

WHO, INCIDENTALLY, I LIKE VERY MUCH.

THEN WHY ARE YOU HIDING IN HERE?

SO DO I, BUT...

AH, I KNOW YOU'VE BEEN DISAPPOINTED BEFORE, SISTER, BUT THIS ONE'S DIFFERENT SOMEHOW. I CAN FEEL IT.

I GUESS I JUST... HE HASN'T MADE HIS INTENTIONS CLEAR...

HIS ATTENTIONS ATTEST TO HIS INTENTIONS.

I JUST THINK IT WOULD BE FOOLISH TO GET MY HOPES UP.

THEN THE WHOLE PARISH IS FOOLISH, BECAUSE THE WHOLE PARISH'S HOPES ARE UP!

I LEFT THE KITCHEN AND DRIFTED BACK TOWARD THE PARTY. NIGHT HAD FALLEN DURING MY ABSENCE.

I'M TOLD TODAY'S YOUR BIRTHDAY.

MN.

SO HOW'S IT FEEL TO BE IN DOUBLE DIGITS AT LAST? HAS IT CHANGED YOUR LIFE DRAMATICALLY?

YES.

WELL... WHAT? IT HAS?

I THINK I'VE STARTED LIKING BOYS.

OH, WELL, CONGRATULATIONS. I CAN THINK OF A FEW WORTH LIKING.

NO, YOU DON'T UNDERSTAND. IT'S TERRIBLE! I'M TURNING INTO SUSA!

I THOUGHT YOU LIKED SUSA.

I DO, BUT... ALL SHE EVER TALKS ABOUT ANY MORE IS BOYS.

128

AND NO SOONER HAD I SAID IT, THAN THERE SHE WAS, AND HE OFF TO MEET HER.

I WATCHED THEM FOR A TIME AND BEGAN TO SEE THAT HE WAS RIGHT, THAT BECOMING SUSA WAS NOT INEVITABLE...

BECAUSE THERE WAS NIESTA, IN HER WORK DRESS AND HEADCLOTH, HER HANDS STILL RED FROM WASHING DISHES...

AND THERE WAS LALO, WHO VERY PLAINLY LOVED HER, NOT CARING WHETHER SHE HAD REFINED MANNERS OR ROUGED LIPS.

IT WAS BEAUTIFUL

TO SEE OUR NIESTA HAPPY.

NOT THAT **I** WAS HAPPY. IN FACT, I WAS MOPEY.

NOBODY LIKES ME. I MIGHT AS WELL FIND A CONVENT AND TURN MYSELF IN **NOW**.

HEY UGH-LEE! ANYBODY SITTING HERE?

OH YEZ. THIS IS **JUST** WHAT I NEED.

WHEW! FINALLY PUT HELOISE TO BED. THAT CHILD COULD OUTRUN ALL THE SAINTS IN HEAVEN, **AND** THEIR DOGS!

MRPH.

HEY, WHAT'S WRONG WITH **YOU**? NEVER KNOWN YOU TO SULK AT A NIGHTFEST BEFORE.

OH, IS **THAT** ALL.

I HAVE A BROKEN... TOE.

NO...

I TOLD HIM. I LEANED RIGHT OVER AND TOLD HIM WHAT I HADN'T TOLD ANYBODY, EVEN THOUGH I COULD TELL AS I SAID IT THAT IT WASN'T TRUE ANYMORE.

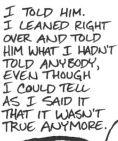

TRIG? REALLY?

I EXPECTED HIM TO LAUGH. I WAS ALMOST HOPING HE'D LAUGH SO I COULD KEEP ON FEELING SORRY FOR MYSELF.

BUT THEN, WHEN HAS BRAN EVER DONE WHAT I EXPECTED?

YOU KNOW, I AM AN EXPERT ON TRIG, HAVING SHARED A ROOM FOR NINE YEARS, AND BELIEVE ME, YOU DON'T WANT **HIM.**

I DON'T?

HE'S AN AMAZING BED-HOG, HIS FEET SMELL LIKE A GOAT SHED, HE SNORES LIKE THERE'S NO TOMORROW...

...AND IF YOU SO MUCH AS **TOUCH** ANY OF HIS STUFF, HE'LL GIVE YOU A NOOGIE!

A WHO?

LIKE THIS! BUT WORSE!

GAH! OKAY! OKAY!

WHAT A CLOD!

I'LL SAY! BUT C'MON AND LET'S JOIN THIS REEL. IT'LL GET YOUR MIND OFF THINGS.

I REALLY CAN'T. MY TOE.

OH, RIGHT. WELL, WE'LL JUST DO A TWO-FOOT.

THIS ISN'T TWO-FOOT MUSIC!

NO, SEE, YOU HOP AROUND ON YOUR GOOD FOOT, AND I'LL HOP AROUND ON ONE FOOT TOO, WHICH TOGETHER MAKES **TWO FEET...**

YOU KNOW I'M RIGHT!

I DON'T KNOW WHEN I'VE LAUGHED SO HARD OR BEEN SO GRATEFUL FOR BRAN'S CHEERFULNESS. I BET WE WERE THE ENVY OF THE WHOLE PARTY — NOBODY HAD AS MUCH FUN AS WE DID.

WHETHER I REALIZED IT THEN OR NOT, BRAN WAS A GOOD FRIEND. WHATEVER THAT SUMMER MAY HAVE BROUGHT OR TAKEN AWAY, THAT'S THE MOMENT I WANT TO KEEP — HOPPING AND LAUGHING LONG INTO THE NIGHT, SILLY OLD BRAN AND ME.

Chapter 5
Of Love & Danger

Concerning the wedding of Pearl-Agnes Fortellga and Bartolo, Duke of Limongello. Try not to cry.

Marry a goat,
Live in manure.

Rupa' proverb

My struggle never ends, Pau-Henoa.

Tell my people
I am lost,
And that I loved them,
But they would not know
Belondweg if they
saw her now.

I am transformed...

THIS IS PRETTY DRESS, ANH? TOO BAD YOU HAVE ONLY CRABBY FACE TO WEAR WITH IT.

Of Love and Danger

PEARL-AGNES WAS CLEVER TO PUT US UP IN TOWN THE NIGHT BEFORE.

I DON'T **EVEN** WANT TO GO TO THIS...

YOU? **YOU**?! SHE IS LIKE MY **SISTER** TO ME! HOW I CAN **BEAR** TO SEE HER..?

I CAN'T BEGIN TO IMAGINE HOW CRABBY WE'D HAVE BEEN IF WE'D COME ALL THE WAY FROM EDDY BROOK.

ALL **RIGHT**, YOU TWO! SHE'S GOING TO GET MARRIED WHETHER YOU'RE THERE OR NOT. I WOULD THINK YOU'D RATHER BE THERE WITH HER.

THE HOUSE PUT A BRAVE FACE FORWARD, ANYWAY. SO WOULD SHE.

SO SHOULD WE.

FOR TELL GAS

140

AH, IT'S EASY TO GET SIDETRACKED. THE COUNTRYFOLK HERE ARE SO TALKATIVE AND FULL OF CURIOSITIES... IT MUST BE LIKE HAVING A GREAT BANQUET SPREAD BEFORE YOU...

OF KNOWLEDGE. A... A BANQUET OF KNOWLEDGE.

SORRY!

HEH-HEH. IT'S OKAY.

MY YOUNGEST, PATE, HAD SCHOLARLY ASPIRATIONS, BUT HE WAS SUCH A ONE TO GET DISTRACTED! OH, HE'D START OUT EAGER AS A COW TO THE MILKING BARN...

...ONLY TO END UP GETTING SILLY OVER SOME GIRL AND FORGETTING HIS STUDIES ALTOGETHER.

AT LEAST YOU CAN'T HAVE **THAT** PROBLEM.

HE TURNED ABRUPTLY, ALARMINGLY PALE.

I THOUGHT HE WAS CHOKING AT FIRST, BUT HE MADE NO MOTION TOWARD HIS THROAT...

HE MADE NO MOTION AT ALL FOR A MINUTE OR TWO. DAME OKRA KEPT CHATTING AWAY LIKE SHE HADN'T NOTICED.

A DIM, SICK FEAR CAME OVER ME... I ALMOST UNDERSTOOD HIS EXPRESSION ... IT WAS ON THE TIP OF MY TONGUE...

SO OF COURSE, THAT'S WHEN FOUGHFAUGH MATERIALIZED.

OMIGOSH! YOU'RE SOOO LUCKY!

C'MON, YOUNG SQUIRREL.

BUT... UH... I...UH...

UH-HUH. ME, TOO. BUT WE CAN'T PUT IT OFF ANY LONGER.

MAKE WAY! MAKE W

143

144

LONG AS HER GREAT HALL WAS, I KEPT WISHING IT WERE LONGER.
BUT NO, IT LOOKED LIKE WE REALLY WERE GOING TO MAKE IT
ALL THE WAY DOWN TO THE MARRYING END.

WH— WHERE ARE YOUR WITNESSES?

THEY ACCOMPANY ME.

THESE...? I HAVE BUT ONE BLOOD RELATION. I BELIEVE I AM ENTITLED TO CHOOSE MY REMAINING WITNESSES.

YES, BUT THEY'RE ...NOT MALE.

PATER, PROCEED.

AND SO HE BEGAN THE CEREMONY, ASKING PEARL-AGNES' "GUARDIAN" THE SAME QUESTION THAT HAS BEGUN COUNTLESS GENERATIONS OF GOREDDI WEDDINGS:

DOES THIS MAIDEN 'FREELY' AND OF HER OWN VOLITION CONSENT TO THIS UNION?

149

I HAVE HERE DOCUMENTATION PROVING THAT THIS WOMAN, **PEARL-AGNES FORTELLGA,** IS ALREADY **MARRIED** TO HER SECOND COUSIN, **MAURIZIO VIZENTE YANN-FAÑCH ST. BAZILLE DE FOUGHFAUGH!** MY SQUIRE!

I AM?!?

WISHT! JUST SMILE AND NOD.

PLEASE PERUSE THIS CONTRACT, ONE AND ALL! DATED JULY 15th, TWO YEARS AGO!

OFFICIATED BY ONE FATHER NIALL DUCANAHAN OF ST. KATHANDA'S PARISH...

FATHER NIALL?

YOU KNOW HIM, PATER?

KNEW HIM IN HIS SEMINARY DAYS. MOST UPSTANDING YOUNG MAN.

INDEED!

...WITNESSED BY SIR CUTHBERTE PETTIBONE (THAT'S ME), THE PIOUS AND MEEK WIDOW SAMPANDER...

X—(mark of Sir Cuth
X—(mark of the W
⊕ (mark of
BAM DUC

AND "BARN PUCNHN?"

BRAN DUCANAHAN. BROTHER TO THE PRIEST.

NIALL OFTEN SPOKE OF A BROTHER. HE'S A FREE FARMER, I BELIEVE?

YE-ES... A MOST RESPECT-ABLE WITNESS.

I'M SURE I'LL REGRET ASKING, BUT WHY HAS NO ONE HEARD OF THIS BEFORE NOW?

AN EXCELLENT QUESTION FROM HER EXCELLENCE! PEARL-AGNES NEVER MENTIONED HER FIRST MARRIAGE BECAUSE IT WAS A HORRIBLE **EMBARRASSMENT!**

THE CHARMING YOUNG FELLOW WAS NOT WHAT HE SEEMED! SHE THOUGHT HE HAD LAND! ASSETS! VIRTUES! A SENSE OF HUMOR!

ANY-THING!

BUT IT TURNS OUT HE'S A BANISHED MAN WHO LIVES IN A MUDDY CAVE!

FORGOT TO MENTION IT! SILLY ME!

IT WAS A CLASSIC CASE OF MARRIAGE UNDER FALSE PRETENSES! WHO CAN TELL ME THE LEGAL STATUS OF SUCH A MARRIAGE?

WAAAAAH! HE'S MARRIED!

A MARRIAGE CONTRACTED UNDER FALSE PRETENSES IS VOID!

CORRECT! GIVE THAT CLEVER LAD A BISCUIT!

BUT NOW I HAVE A QUESTION FOR PATER NOSEWORTHY.

GURK...

TELL ME, PATER— IS A VOID MARRIAGE AUTOMATICALLY VOID...

..OR DOES THE CHURCH HAVE TO BE INVOLVED IN SOME WAY?

WELL...

TECHNICALLY, SHE SHOULD HAVE PETITIONED THE BISHOP FOR AN ANNULLMENT— WHICH HE WOULD HAVE UNDOUBTEDLY GRANTED IN A CASE LIKE THIS...

WHERE IS HE GOING WITH THIS?

BUT IF THE MARRIAGE HAD BEEN ANNULLED, WOULD THIS CONTRACT STILL EXIST?

WELL, NO...

YOU'LL SEE.

THE MAN'S A MAD GENIUS.

SO! RATHER THAN GETTING HER MARRIAGE FORMALLY ANNULLED, PEARL-AGNES SIMPLY ASSUMED IT WAS VOID, AND THEREFORE FELT NO NEED TO MENTION IT TO YOU SUPERCILIOUS BUSYBODIES!

BUT SHE COULD HAVE IT ANNULLED THIS MINUTE, IF SHE WISHES. IT'S USUALLY UP TO THE BISHOP, BUT THE QUEEN MAY CERTAINLY PERFORM SUCH AN OFFICE.

INDEED.

154

A WIDOW.

YESSS!

EXACTLY! A WIDOW! NOW WE ALL KNOW WHAT HAPPENS WHEN A DAUGHTER INHERITS — THAT'S WHY WE'RE HERE TODAY — BUT WHAT ABOUT A WIDOW? MAGISTRATES? WHO CAN TELL ME?

NO TAKERS? WELL THEN *I'LL* TELL YOU — A WIDOW CAN **KEEP** HER PROPERTY!

LOOK AT THIS POOR GRIEVING WOMAN! WOULD YOU DEPRIVE HER OF HER LAST MEAGER SUPPORT AND LEAVE HER DESTITUTE?

LET IT NEVER BE SAID THAT THE GOREDDI PEOPLE DEPRIVED AN HONORABLE WIDOW OF HER LIVELIHOOD! ORPHANS, SURE, BUT **NEVER** WIDOWS!

ONCE THE PRISONERS WERE TAKEN AWAY, THE PARTY DWINDLED TO JUST PEARL'S CLOSEST FRIENDS. WE ALL RELOCATED TO THE KITCHEN TO HELP EAT THE GRAND WEDDING SUPPER GERTHE HAD MADE.

PEARL-AGNES FINALLY LOST HER COMPOSURE.

I-I CAN'T BELIEVE... I ALMOST...M-MARRIED B-B-B...

IT IS OVER NOW.

I W-WOULD HAVE DONE IT, T-TOO!

YOU WERE BRAVE, MY PEARL

AND M-MAURIZIO...! HE W-WENT TO PRISON FOR M-ME! :SOB.!: HOW C-COULD I LET HIM DO THAT?

AH, NOW THAT'S SOMETHING WE CAN EASE YOUR MIND ABOUT. YOUR COUSIN ISN'T SUFFERING UNDULY.

HE AND UNCLE CUTHBERTE LAND IN JAIL EVERY OTHER MONTH. THEY'VE GOT THEIR OWN CELL WITH THEIR NAMES ON IT.

:SNIF: HEH. THAT BOY!

SOON SHE JOINED US AROUND THE FIRE

WHY DIDN'T YOU JUST MARRY YOUR COUSIN TO BEGIN WITH?

I WON'T SAY IT NEVER OCCURRED TO ME. BUT A BANISHED MAN — YES, I **DID** KNOW — CAN'T LEGALLY MARRY, PERIOD.

GOOD THING THE QUEEN DIDN'T POINT THAT OUT!

OH, SHE WOULD HAVE, FOR ANYONE BUT MAURIZIO. HE WAS 8 WHEN THEY WERE BANISHED. SHE KNOWS HE DIDN'T DESERVE IT.

HEE-HEE! AND THAT MARRIAGE LICENCE! HOW FAKE WAS THAT?

BUT NOBODY DARED SPEAK AGAINST IT AFTER THE PATER VOUCHED FOR THE PRIEST! PERFECT! AND WHO ELSE COULD'VE EXPOSED THE FRAUD?

I COULD HAVE.

IT WAS DATED 2 YEARS AGO, BUT 2 YEARS AGO BRAN COULDN'T HAVE SIGNED HIS OWN NAME!

HA! HE BARELY CAN NOW!

WE LAUGHED AND TALKED LATE INTO THE NIGHT.

I WAS PLANNING TO SPILL INK ALL OVER THE CONTRACT!

I WAS GOING TO DUMP OATNOG DOWN HIS DOUBLET!

WHAT A LOT OF NAUGHTY GIRLS I'VE GOT!

ONLY BRIEFLY DID IT STRIKE ME THAT LALO WASN'T THERE. THIS WAS EXACTLY THE SORT OF GATHERING HE'D ENJOY.

WHEN DID HE LEAVE?

SO WHA ARE YO GOING T DO TO CELEB

I DON'T KNOW! I HADN'T COUNT ON BEING A WIDOW SO

BUT THERE WAS NO PLACE IN THAT KITCHEN FOR WORRY. I FORGOT ALL ABOUT HIM.

OUCH! I'M GOING TO HAVE TO WEAR ONE OF THOSE UGLY LITTLE CAPS FOR A YEAR, AREN'T I.

A SMALL PRICE TO PAY!

MOIRA, GO GET ONE!

HA HA HA!

MAKE HER WEAR IT!

WHAT WE DIDN'T KNOW, LAUGHING AND TALKING AROUND PEARL-
AGNES' HEARTH THAT NIGHT, IS THAT CULLEN DUCANAHAN HAD
BROUGHT HOME A WIFE.
    HER NAME WAS FLORA AND SHE WAS FIFTEEN YEARS OLD.
SHE DIDN'T STAND A CHANCE.

Chapter 6

In Her Eyes

Wherein many things end, and others begin.
Go on now – what're you reading <u>this</u> for?

... But I, unfortunate, have seen
The flash of love and danger in her eyes.
Why then, Maeta, do you feign surprise
If I must where she bids me go?

Belondweg, book XVII
The Confession of General Orison

In Her Eyes

...FOREVER AND EVER. AMEN.

AMEN.

AMEN.

IT'S A PITY YOU NEVER KNEW HER, BRAN. SHE WAS A WONDERFUL PERSON.

KIND, UNSELFISH, AND BEAUTIFUL, THOUGH SHE DIDN'T KNOW IT. SHE MADE GREAT CHEESE, AND WOULD SING WHILE SHE WORKED IF SHE THOUGHT NO ONE WAS LISTENING.

HEH-HEH. YEAH.

SHE KEPT THE WHOLE FARM IN ORDER, ESPECIALLY US BOYS. WE'D GRUMBLE ABOUT HOW STRICT SHE WAS, BUT TRUTHFULLY, SHE DID AN AWFUL LOT FOR US THAT WE NEVER NOTICED OR APPRECIATED, THAT WE SHOULD HAVE THANKED HER FOR BEFORE IT WAS TOO LATE.

MMM. YEAH.

I ACCIDENTALLY LET THE BULL LOOSE ONCE— IT TOOK 5 MEN TO BRING HIM ALL THE WAY BACK FROM ST. PASTRY'S. CULLEN TORE AROUND LOOKING FOR WHO'D DONE IT. IT WAS JUST A MATTER OF TIME BEFORE HE GOT TO ME. I DUCKED INTO THE KITCHEN JUST AHEAD OF HIM.

167

"SHE NEEDS YOUR HELP NOW AS SURELY AS YOU'VE NEEDED HERS..."

ALL WAS NOT WELL WITH NIESTA.

MA RUSHED OVER THE MINUTE SHE HEARD CULLEN HAD MAR-RIED, AND CAME BACK SATISFIED.

SHE IS MOST TIMID, THIS WIFE. IT WILL BE NOTHING ON NIESTA.

WE'D FEARED ILL-WILL BETWEEN THE WOMEN, BUT TRUTHFULLY, FLORA FOUND THE HEN-HOUSE MORE MENACING THAN HER NEW SISTER-IN-LAW.

um... um... nice chicky!

EVEN CULLEN'S ATTEMPTS TO PIT THEM AGAINST EACH OTHER SEEMED TO FALL FLAT.

FLORA COOKS MY DINNER FROM NOW ON!

ALL RIGHT.

IT'S HER WIFELY PRIVILEGE! THE KITCHEN IS HERS NOW! YOU HAVE NO RIGHT TO IT!

OKAY.

eep!

AND FRANKLY, SUCH MANEUVERS GOT HIM WHAT HE DESERVED. FLORA, BLESS HER HEART, DIDN'T KNOW WHICH WAY WAS UP IN A KITCHEN.

oh! oh!

WE WERE SO RELIEVED THINGS WEREN'T WORSE THAT IT TOOK US LONGER THAN IT SHOULD HAVE TO NOTICE THE DULLNESS IN HER EYES.

thanks for killing me a chicken, sister! who knew they were so m-mean?

we won't tell Cullen, right?

SHE WITHDREW. SHE HARDLY SPOKE TO ANYONE.

how do i get the feathers off?

I'LL TEACH YOU!

SHE WOULDN'T EVEN SCOLD BRAN FOR PREYING ON FLORA'S CREDULOUS SIMPLICITY, AGAIN AND AGAIN.

YOU'VE GOT TO BITE 'EM OFF. USE YOUR TEETH!

oh, okay! thank you, Bran!

i'm glad you don't still hate me!

TRIG FIGURED IT OUT FIRST—"HER OLLIE'S UP AND ABANDONED HER."

INDEED, LALO HADN'T SHOWN HIS FACE AT NEWGROVE SINCE BEFORE PEARL'S WEDDING.

OH, HE'D BEEN SEEN IN TOWN, BUT HE WAS CLEARLY AND POINTEDLY AVOIDING NIESTA.

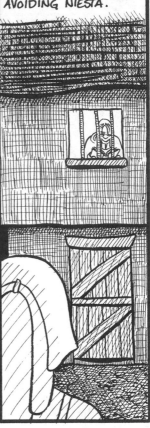

TRIG SAID SHE'D GONE SO FAR AS TO SEEK LALO OUT AT THE WIDOW SAMPANDER'S...

...WHERE SHE WAS TOLD (RUDELY, IF I KNOW THE WIDOW) THAT HE WOULDN'T SEE HER, AND THAT SHE WAS NOT TO COME AGAIN.

NO REASON GIVEN. NOTHING. NO WONDER SHE WAS DRIFTING AROUND BLANKLY, AS THOUGH SHE'D BEEN SLAPPED.

NIALL CAME TO DINNER SEVERAL NIGHTS RUNNING TO TALK ABOUT HER.

THIS CAN'T CONTINUE!

THAT SON OF SEVEN GOATS!

SPLORT!

THE MORE DESPONDENT SHE GROWS, THE MORE AUTHORITY CULLEN STRIPS FROM HER. SHE WON'T EVEN PROTEST!

I FIND THIS OLLPHEIST, I BREAK HIS FINGERS!

WE'VE GOT TO GET HER OUT OF THAT HOUSE, THAT'S ALL THERE IS TO IT.

BUT I DON'T SEE ANY ALTERNATIVE TO A CONVENT. SHE'S NOT GOING TO BE HAPPY ABOUT IT.

WELL, NOW, IT'S NOT AN UNPLEASANT LIFE, I HEAR. THEY EVEN MAKE CHEESE AT ST. AGNYESTA'S IN EDWINSTOWE...

BUT... BUT..!

SO IT HAPPENED THAT WHEN NIALL URGED BRAN TO HELP HIS SISTER, IT OCCURRED TO ME THAT **I** COULD HELP. I RAN TO THE WIDOW SAMPANDER'S INSTEAD OF GOING HOME.

SURELY THIS IS ALL A BIG MISUNDERSTANDING...

E. L.

AMY!

WHAT A NICE SURPRISE!

COME IN!

PARDON THE MESS! I SEEM TO ACQUIRE A LOT OF STUFF ON THESE RESEARCH TRIPS, AND THEN I HAVE TO SORT IT ALL BEFORE I CAN PACK...

Y-YOU'RE LEAVING?

NEW TERM STARTS SEPTEMBER 1ST. I'M TEACHING A CLASS THIS QUARTER.

HAVE A SEAT.

I WAS STUNNED. WHATEVER PLAN I'D HAD COMING IN (AND IT WASN'T MUCH OF A PLAN) FLEW RIGHT OUT OF MY HEAD.

UH... IT'S BEEN SO LONG SINCE I'VE SEEN YOU. IT WAS AT PEARL'S...

YES, I'VE HAD TO DO A LOT OF LAST MINUTE RUSHING AROUND TO GET MY DATA. I THINK I FINALLY GOT ENOUGH TO DO A SOLID PRELIMINARY ANALYSIS THIS WINTER...

BISCUITS?

BARLEY WATER?

THIS WASN'T WORKING! I COULDN'T COME UP WITH A GOOD LEAD-IN...

THEN I'LL SUBMIT A FORMAL PROPOSAL TO MY COMMITTEE...

NG. I'LL DRINK OUT OF THIS ONE.

I SWALLOWED HARD AND JUMPED RIGHT TO THE CRISIS:

WHAT ABOUT NIESTA?

WHAT **ABOUT** HER?

WELL, IT'S JUST THAT... UH... SHE... YOU... I MEAN...

AW, PHOOEY!

ALL RIGHT, LISTEN. I KNOW THERE WERE LOTS OF RUMORS AND EX--PECTATIONS CIRCULATING, PEOPLE SAYING I WAS GOING TO MARRY NIESTA OR SOME SUCH NONSENSE.

BUT, FACT IS, I **CAN'T** MARRY NIESTA.

WHAT? WHY NOT?

FIRST OF ALL, IT'S ILLEGAL, UNDER BOTH DRAGONLAW AND THE LAWS OF GOREDD. IN FACT, GOREDD HAS FIVE SEPARATE LAWS FORBIDDING IT.

FIVE. ONE WOULDN'T DO, APPARENTLY. THAT SHOULD TELL YOU A THING OR TWO ABOUT PUBLIC SENTIMENT.

BUT HE'S STILL A CATTLE BEAST, WHETHER SHE LOVES HIM OR NOT...

AND IT WOULD ONLY BE CRUEL TO LET HER CONTINUE.

BUT... DO YOU REALLY THINK YOU CAN COME UP WITH AN OBJECTION I HAVEN'T THOUGHT OF ALREADY?

YOU'RE GOING TO SAY MAYBE SHE DOESN'T WANT CHILDREN. I'M TOLD SUCH HUMANS EXIST. LET'S SAY SHE IS. AND LET'S JUST SAY SHE'S NEITHER HORRIFIED NOR REPULSED WHEN SHE LEARNS WHAT I REALLY AM...

OOH! AND LET'S PRETEND, WHILE WE'RE AT IT, THAT WE FIND SOME LEGAL LOOPHOLE, OVERLOOKED FOR CENTURIES, SO IT'S NOT COMPLETELY ILLEGAL! CAN YOU WRAP YOUR IMAGINATION AROUND ALL THAT?

WELL GUESS WHAT! I **STILL** COULDN'T MARRY NIESTA!

I AM A GRAD STUDENT! I LIVE IN A COMMON HOUSE WITH FIFTEEN OTHER DRAGONS! WHAT KIND OF EXISTENCE CAN I POSSIBLY OFFER HER? WHAT WOULD SHE DO ALL DAY?

176

ALL I REMEMBER IS THAT I RAN. I RAN AND RAN AND RAN...

I'VE RUINED EVERYTHING!

I'VE RUINED EVERYTHING...

...AS IF MAYBE THE MOTION OF MY BODY COULD TURN OFF MY BRAIN.

I'VE RUINED... I'VE RUINED... I'VE...

RUINED...

IT DIDN'T QUITE WORK. I GOT HOME PRETTY FAST, THOUGH.

EVERY...

THING...

OW!

DAME OKRA WAS THERE, HAVING A MUG OF BUTTERMILK AND A GOSSIP WITH MA.

NOTHING LIKE SUMMER TO BRING HANDSOME NE'ER-DO-WELLS OUT OF THE WOODWORK. I DO **NOT** MISS BEING YOUNG!

YOU KNOW HOW IT ENDS.

GASP!

HE RUNS OFF AT THE FIRST BREATH OF AUTUMN.

POOF! GONE! NOT EVEN A WORD TO HER.

OH... CACK.

IT **WASN'T** JUST INDIGESTION!

NAHULLA... BY ST. SPADILLA! I DON'T KNOW HOW TO TELL YOU THIS. I COULD HAVE PREVENTED THIS WHOLE THING...

HAH! YOU KNEW HE DID THIS BEFORE, ANH?

NO. **NO**. QUITE THE OPPOSITE. THIS IS A VERY UNFORTUNATE SITUATION, FOR REASONS YOU'RE NOT EVEN AWARE OF.

HE BETRAYED WITH HER! HE PRETENDED TO LOVE HER!

OH, I'M SURE HE **DOES** LOVE HER. ~:SIGH:~ THE PROBLEM IS, HE'S NOT SUPPOSED TO.

HE'S A DRAGON, NAHULLA.

HE'ETZUMEKHE..?

I WILL EAT HIS HEART!

OBOY.

179

Panel 1: I DON'T KNOW HOW WE CALMED HER DOWN, BUT WE FINALLY DID.

I FEEL JUST TERRIBLE ABOUT ALL THIS, NAHULLA, AND I'D LIKE TO MAKE AMENDS TO THIS GIRL.

IT IS NOT ON YOU.

Panel 2: NO, I COULD HAVE TOLD YOU WHAT HE WAS AT THE VERY BEGINNING OF THE SUMMER. I JUST ASSUMED YOU KNEW.

Panel 3: I AM IN A POSITION TO HELP, AND IT **WILL** BE ON ME IF I DON'T DO WHAT I CAN. LET ME SPEAK WITH HER BROTHER, THE PRIEST.

Panel 4: I FETCHED NIALL FOR HER. THEY TALKED A LONG TIME.

IT WILL BE EASIEST TO HEAR IT FROM YOU.

AGREED. I DON'T THINK SHE'LL GO FOR THIS PLAN OF YOURS, THOUGH.

Panel 5: SHE DOESN'T HAVE TO. I JUST WANT HER TO KNOW SHE HAS A CHOICE. THE WORLD IS NOT CLOSED TO HER YET.

Panel 6: NIALL BROUGHT NIESTA OVER THE NEXT DAY AND TALKED TO HER OUT IN THE GARDEN. BRAN CAME ALONG AND BUGGED ME WHILE I DID MY CHORES.

SHE'S REALLY SCARED OF CHICKENS, SO I PUT ONE IN HER TRUNK...

...AND I'VE BEEN PUTTING TOADS IN ALL THE CUPBOARDS. I'M GONNA START ON SNAKES SOON IF SHE DOESN'T RUN AWAY.

BRAN, THAT'S MEAN.

SO? ONCE SHE'S GONE NIESTA CAN BE HAPPY AGAIN.

SHE'S NOT SAD ABOUT FLORA! SHE'S SAD ABOUT OLLIE!

WELL, DUH! BUT YOU KNOW WHAT I NOTICED? HE STOPPED COMING THE VERY DAY FLORA ARRIVED!

YEAH, SO?

WELL OBVIOUSLY, HE CAN'T STAND HER EITHER!

WE GET RID OF FLORA, OLLIE COMES BACK, NIESTA'S HAPPY AGAIN. SIMPLE AS THAT.

I JUST ASSUMED YOU'D WANT TO THINK IT OVER A LITTLE LONGER!

NO, YOU JUST ASSUMED I'D PREFER YOUR CONVENT IDEA. WELL I DON'T!

BUT IT WASN'T AS SIMPLE AS THAT. I WANTED TO TELL HIM, BUT THE WORDS WOULDN'T PASS MY THROAT. THEY SAT LIKE A LUMP ON MY HEART.

...I CAN'T FIGURE OUT WHAT KIND OF FAMILY FLORA'S FROM. NOT FARMERS, THAT'S FOR SURE...

FORGIVE HIM, IF YOU CAN.

NOW COME MEET PHYLLIDA AND LOUCA.

VERY HAPPY!

《HEY! SHE'S PRETTIER THAN I THOUGHT SHE'D BE. WE SHOULD FIX HER UP WITH COUSIN FOUAD!》

《LOUCA, SHUT **UP**!》

I HAVE PACKED FOR YOU SOME FOOD, ANH? AND YOU TAKE VERY GOOD CARE ON HER! SHE IS MY SISTER!

FA**LA!** HOW WILL I BEAR IT?

NAHULLA...

AND NIESTA, I HAVE SOME MONEY FOR YOU.

I'VE BEEN SETTING IT ASIDE. IT WAS TO HAVE BEEN YOUR D-DOWRY.

I'LL MISS YOU.

YOU'RE ALWAYS WELCOME BACK.

A LITTLE HELP HERE!

HOPE WE HAVEN'T HELD YOU UP. CAPTAIN ZONKUS HERE COULD SLEEP THROUGH TH' END OF THE WORLD.

HEY, SLEEPY-HEAD. BRAN, HONEY, WAKE UP.

MMMGH. GUH! HOW COME AMY'S HERE?

OF COURSE, NO ONE HAD TOLD BRAN WHAT WAS GOING ON.

WH...WH..? I WAS GOOD! I DIDN'T... WHY ARE YOU...?

I WAS HELPING!

BRAN.

BRAN...

AND THEN BRAN WAS CRYING AND EVERYBODY WAS CRYING AND I JUST COULDN'T WATCH. I JUST COULDN'T.

AMY!

Pst! AMY!

184

I'LL SHOW YOU.

I'VE HAD DREAMS LIKE THIS, WHERE I'M RUNNING THROUGH THE DEWY, FLINTY FIELDS IN MY NIGHTDRESS BEFORE THE SUN IS FULLY UP.

I DIDN'T EVEN HAVE MY SHOES ON. HE TOOK ME ON HIS BACK.

HE WAS FAST. I TOOK HIM ON THE FOOTPATH THAT CROSSES SHORT RIDGE...

...AND COMES OUT SOUTH OF LITTLE ASHCROFT...

...RIGHT ONTO THE WESTERN ROAD. WE WAITED A LONG TIME.

YOU'RE SURE THIS IS THE ROAD.

UH... GETTING LESS SURE.

188

IS THIS SEAT TAKEN?

NO.

WHAT'RE YOU DOING BACK? I THOUGHT YOU WENT TO PORPHYRY.

NO, JUST PART WAY, TO HELP HER MAKE THE TRANSITION.

I THOUGHT YOU'D GO RIGHT BACK TO SCHOOL FROM THERE.

MN. NOT SUPER ANXIOUS TO GET BACK AT THIS POINT. BESIDES, I HAD SOME UNFINISHED BUSINESS HERE. I HAD TO BE SURE ALL WAS RIGHT WITH A PARTICULAR YOUNG FRIEND OF MINE.

I'M NOT MAD AT YOU, IF THAT'S WHAT YOU MEAN.

THAT'S PART OF IT. BUT YOU DESERVE A BETTER EXPLANATION THAN YOU'VE GOTTEN SO FAR. I WAS COMPLETELY OUT OF LINE IN BLOWING UP AT YOU THE WAY I DID. PLEASE KNOW I WAS MOSTLY ANGRY AT MYSELF.

WHY? AMONG DRAGONS THERE'S A TERRIBLE TABOO AGAINST... ATTACHMENT TO HUMAN WOMEN. IT'S CONSIDERED A SHAMEFUL ILLNESS.

SO I SPENT THE SUMMER TELLING MYSELF I COULDN'T **POSSIBLY** BE... AFFLICTED. NO WAY. "OH, I'M JUST BEING NEIGHBORLY AND HELPING HER WITH HOLY MOW."

"SHE'S A GREAT SOURCE OF FOLKLORE" (IN FACT, SHE **IS**).

"HER BROTHER'S SO ORNERY! SHE NEEDS A FRIEND!"

OOH, AND MY FAVORITE — "TALKING TO HER HELPS CLARIFY MY THOUGHTS ON THE RESEARCH." UH-HUH! THAT'S RICH!

THEN, AT PEARL'S... I SAW THAT! A REALIZATION LIKE A KNIFE IN THE GUT. NOT ONLY HAD **I** GONE SERIOUSLY ASTRAY, I HAD LED NIESTA **ON**...

I PANICKED. I CUT OFF ALL CONTACT WITH HER, FIGURING SHE'D GET OVER ME WITHOUT TOO MUCH TROUBLE. I'M NOT **THAT** REMARKABLE.

I COULDN'T BE HER LOVER, BUT I COULD HAVE BEEN A FRIEND WHEN SHE NEEDED ONE THE MOST.

... I FAILED HER IN THAT.

NIESTA, WHOM I CARED VERY MUCH ABOUT.

SO, OF COURSE, THAT'S WHEN CULLEN GETS MARRIED, AND SHE HAS TO FACE THAT AND MY DESERTION SIMULTANEOUSLY.

THAT'S OK. I'M TALKING ABOUT THE BEGINNING. WHAT HAPPENS AT THE VERY BEGINNING OF BELONDWEG?

HERE. BLOW YOUR NOSE.

THE MORDONDEY KILL HER DA AND BURN...

SGRONX!

NOT QUITE. THAT HAPPENS BEFORE THE BEGINNING. WHEN WE FIRST SEE BELONDWEG, HER FATHER'S DEAD. HER CITY'S BURNT. SHE'S OUT ON THE PLAIN CRYING.

YEAH, OKAY.

NOW SAY YOU WERE BELONDWEG AT THAT MOMENT. RIGHT THEN. IF SOMEBODY ASKED YOU, WOULD YOU SAY YOU WERE AT THE BEGINNING OR THE END OF A STORY?

IT... IT WOULD FEEL LIKE THE END OF EVERYTHING!

EXACTLY. BUT FOR US, READING THE BOOK, IT'S DIFFERENT. WE KNOW IT'S THE START OF THE BOOK. WE CAN SEE PAU HENOA WATCHING HER FROM BEHIND THAT BUSH. WE CAN FEEL FROM THE WEIGHT OF THE BOOK THAT THERE'S A LOT OF STORY LEFT TO COME.

oh yeah, **THAT'S** reassuring!

AND REMEMBER WHEN SHE MEETS PAU HENOA? SHE DOESN'T EVEN KNOW WHO HE IS. BUT HE'S ALWAYS THERE, AMY, BEHIND A BUSH OR AROUND THE BEND, WAITING TO LEAD US INTO THE NEXT STORY.

201

YEAH, I WAS THINKING IT TOO — THE MAD BUN'S A SPEEDY CRITTER. LALO HAD A POINT, THOUGH, ABOUT BEGINNINGS. NIESTA AND BRAN WERE OFF TO NEW ADVENTURES, THAT'S FOR SURE. MAYBE WE ALL WERE.

SO LEAD ON, RABBIT-MAN. I AM WITH YOU. LET'S MAKE THIS STORY GO ON AND ON.

HEY, FOUGHFAUGH — HOW DOES BELONDWEG **END**?

I JUST WANT TO KNOW IF I'M READING A COMEDY OR A TRAGEDY.

HEH HEH HEH!

NO, NO. JUST THINKING OF AN EXILE I KNOW.

WHAT, YOU WANT ME TO RUIN IT FOR YOU?

IT'S BOTH. BUT IT ENDS OKAY. AFTER YEARS OF TRIALS AND EXILE SHE COMES BACK AND RETAKES HER COUNTRY.

WAS THAT FUNNY?

I'D LOVE TO WRITE "THE END" RIGHT HERE, BUT THAT'D DEFEAT MY OWN ARGUMENT, NOW WOULDN'T IT. INSTEAD I'LL JUST SAY, "BACK SOON!" THERE'S MORE WHERE THAT CAME FROM.

Scholars love maps!
(Well, *I* love maps anyway.)

Drawn by her scholarliness the dragon Sik in the year 35 of the Comonot. The Provinces of Goredd are holdovers from Belondweg's time, when each would have been a separate kingdom. Goredd's absurdly straight southern border was one of the provisions of the Treaty of the Triad, which also banished the knights.

The Missing Triskele

In my initial design, the cover was to have had the appearance of leather binding with this triskele stamped on it. The illumination won out in the end, but I still like my triskele very much.

"Triskele" is straight from Greek, and means "three-legged." There's another, more traditional one on the very first page and at the top of the *Dramatis Personae*.

What?!?
There are **Amy Unbounded** adventures you don't have?? That's **terrible!**

Fortunately, it's also easy to fix!

As those of you who are clever may have gleaned, *Belondweg Blossoming* was not the first *Amy Unbounded* comic book I ever did. Amy had six short adventures before that, which are still available in minicomic form.

Find out how Amy got her copy of *Belondweg* in the first place! Join her as she has tea with Molly and Susa, dances the "Mean and Stingy Dance" for the Widow Sampander, celebrates the silliest day of the year, gets arrested, becomes a famous bombarde player, and inadvertently participates in the murder of an innocent cheese! Not all in the same episode, thank Allsaints!

I do hope to collect *Amy* #1-6 someday, but you never know – I might get run over by a llama caravan and be unable to work. These things happen. And at $1.50 each, minicomics are cheaper than greeting cards! Plus they have better plots!

Visit www.amyunbounded.com for ordering information, or send us e-mail at amyunbounded@yahoo.com.

About the Authorette

Rigoberta Francesca dei Fagioli was born in 1432 to a family of Neapolitan salt merchants. At the age of 12 she was kidnapped by the rival Pimiento family, and forced into hard labor in the pepper mines. She escaped in 1449 and disappeared from all records until 1467, when she resurfaced abruptly as hairdresser to the notorious Bishop Formiga of Ghent. Upon the bishop's inevitable demise, she taught herself to read, write, swim, and interpret an astrolabe. She composed motets in seven voices, designed an unsinkable dinghy, had holy visions of biscuits and bacon, discovered a cure for the creeping mange, and wrote many, many enraged letters to Torquemada, who apparently owed her money. Rigoberta died in 1488 of heresy, having never produced a comic book in her life.

Rachel Hartman is one up on her already.